VOLUME THREE

VOLUME THREE

RACHEL SMYTHE

NEW YORK

Published in the United States by Del Rey,
an imprint of Random House, a division of
Penguin Random House LLC, New York.

DEL REY and the HOUSE colophon are registered trademarks of Penguin Random House LLC.

Portions of this work originally appeared on Webtoons.com.

Hardcover ISBN 978-0-593-16031-2
Trade Paperback ISBN 978-0-593-35609-8

Printed in China

With thanks to:
Johana R. Ahumada, Yulia Garibova (Hita), Jaki Haboon, Amy Kim,
Kristina Ness, Karen Pavon, M. Rawlings, and Court Rogers

Penguin Random House team:
Ted Allen, Erin Korenko, Sarah Peed, and Elizabeth Schaefer

randomhousebooks.com

2 4 6 8 9 7 5 3 1

First Edition

Book design by Edwin Vazquez

To Jem Yoshioka

An excellent friendship to share a lifetime of stories.

CONTENT WARNING
FROM RACHEL SMYTHE

Lore Olympus regularly deals with themes of physical and mental abuse, sexual trauma, and toxic relationships.

Some of the interactions in this volume may be distressing for some readers. Please exercise discretion, and seek out the support of others if you require it.

SIGH

Looking out for Persephone is so much harder than I thought it was going to be.

MRRRRR

MRRRRR

DUMB BROTHER

Heyyyyyy.

Hey, are you all right?

Ah, I got chewed out by Hestia yesterday.

She's completely overreacted to that stupid tabloid and confiscated Persephone's coat.

Really?

I mean-- really?

...Maybe she was right to be angry.

Excuse me?

I just get the feeling Persephone's not taking her duties very seriously.